So BIG and So Small

by John Coy

illustrated by Steph Lew

beaming  **books**

MINNEAPOLIS

I'm so big

next to a baby,

a puppy,

a squirming kitten.

I'm huge beside a bird,

a butterfly,

a buzzing bumblebee.

I'm gigantic compared to a seashell,

a pebble,

a speck of sand.

But when I go to the zoo,
I'm so small

next to a zebra,

a lion,

a giraffe.

I'm tiny by an oak tree, a waterfall,

a mountain.

I'm teensy-weensy compared to the world, the sun, the sky,

the universe.

I'm so small.

I'm so big.

I'm just right.

For Henry and Lewis. —J.C.

To my Mom and Dad. Also, my Mango,
the best foot warmer anyone could ask for. —S.L.

Text copyright © 2020 John Coy
Illustrations copyright © 2020 Beaming Books

Published in 2020 by Beaming Books, an imprint of 1517 Media.

26 25 24 23 22 21 20   1 2 3 4 5 6 7 8

Hardcover ISBN: 978-1-5064-6058-1
Ebook ISBN: 978-1-5064-6658-3

Library of Congress Cataloging-in-Publication Data

Names: Coy, John, 1958- author. | Lew, Steph, illustrator.
Title: So big and so small / by John Coy ; illustrated by Steph Lew.
Description: Minneapolis, MN : Beaming Books, [2020] | Audience: Ages 3-8.
  | Summary: Illustrations and easy-to-read text capture a child's
  perspective while towering over a baby, a butterfly, and a seashell,
  feeling dwarfed by a giraffe, a waterfall, and the universe, and feeling
  just the right size.
Identifiers: LCCN 2020005040 (print) | LCCN 2020005041 (ebook) | ISBN
  9781506460581 (hardcover) | ISBN 9781506466583 (ebook)
Subjects: CYAC: Size--Fiction.
Classification: LCC PZ7.C839455 So 2020 (print) | LCC PZ7.C839455 (ebook)
  | DDC [E]--dc23
LC record available at https://lccn.loc.gov/2020005040
LC ebook record available at https://lccn.loc.gov/2020005041

VN0004589; 9781506460581; SEPT2020

Beaming Books
510 Marquette Avenue
Minneapolis, MN 55402
Beamingbooks.com

ABOUT THE AUTHOR AND ILLUSTRATOR

 JOHN COY is the author of young adult novels, the 4 for 4 middle-grade series, and numerous picture books, including *On Your Way* and *My Mighty Journey: A Waterfall's Story*. He lives in Minneapolis by the Mississippi River and visits schools around the world.

 STEPH LEW is an artist/illustrator from San Francisco. She graduated from San José State University with a BFA in animation/illustration. When she's not drawing, she enjoys baking, sewing, propagating her succulents, and, especially, taking pictures of her shih tzu, Mango.